The Runaway Soup

and Other Stories

By Michaela Muntean
Illustrated by Tom Cooke

Featuring Jim Henson's Sesame Street Muppets

A Sesame Street/Golden Press Book

Published by Western Publishing Company, Inc.,
in conjunction with Children's Television Workshop

The Runaway Soup

One cold monster morning, Grover woke up and said,
"Today is a day to stay home in bed.

"But, oh, how I wish I had something hot—
A big bowl of soup would just hit the spot!"

Some hot steamy soup in a big roomy dish,
A stream of cream soup was Grover's one wish.

He knew just wishing would not do much good,
But then Grover thought of something that would.

"I will cook up some soup, I will surprise everyone,
And when they wake up, the soup will be done."

So in the biggest big pot he could find
Grover cooked up a soup that was one-of-a-kind.

"I will start with tomatoes, peppers, and peas,
Noodles and celery, peanuts and cheese...

"I will add a few pumpkins, and gooseberry jam,
Some radishes, carrots, some beans, and a yam...

"Some pancakes and pickles might taste very nice,
And what would soup be without adding some rice?"

He stirred it all up with a long wooden spoon,
Then, smiling, he said, "It should be done soon."

That soup started humming inside of the pot.
Then it started growing, and it grew a *lot!*

Over the oven and onto the floor,
That soup started heading right out the front door.

"Stop!" Grover cried. "Please do not run away!"
But that soup would not stop. That soup would not stay.

Oh, that soup-to-go was go, going, gone
On its way out the door and across the front lawn.

It bubbled along in a fat soupy stream
As each monster woke from his own monster dream.

They opened their eyes, they opened their doors,
To find runaway soup had covered their floors.

One monster hollered, and one gave a whoop,
As they all followed Grover's wild runaway soup.

It ran down Main Street and then through the back ways;
It looked like that soup could keep running for days.

But at Sesame Corner, past Alphabet Bend,
That soup missed a turn and it hit a dead end!

The monsters who followed that hot soupy path
Went slipping and sliding into a soup bath!

They had soup in their fur. They had soup-soggy clothes.
They had soup everywhere from their heads to their toes.

"Oh, no," Grover cried, "look at what I have done!"
But his friends only laughed and said, "It's been fun!

"For we've eaten soups with names that sound silly,
Like chowder, and gumbo, and pepper-pot chili,

"But we've never seen, or yet heard about,
A fast soup-to-go that could take itself out!

"So if you decide to make soup again soon,
Remind us to bring a big bowl and a spoon!"

The Runaway Hat

Ernie's favorite hat is the one that Bert gave him.

One spring afternoon Ernie put on his favorite hat and went for a walk in the park. There were tiny new green leaves on the trees. There were red and yellow tulips in the flower beds.

The wind began to blow. At first it was a gentle breeze and soft as a whisper. But then the wind grew stronger, and it blew harder and harder.

Ernie felt a sudden gust and reached up to hold his hat on his head, but he was not as fast as the wind. The wind blew his hat right off his head and lifted it into the air.

"Stop!" Ernie cried as he ran after his hat. "Don't run away, hat!" But his hat did not stop, and the wind did not stop. It blew harder and harder, and it carried Ernie's hat away, higher and higher in the air.

Ernie looked and looked, but he could not find his hat. "It has to be around here somewhere," he said. "Hats do not just disappear!"

It was getting late. Ernie was cold, and tired, and hungry. "Wherever you are, blue hat," Ernie shouted into the wind, "stay there! I will be back to find you tomorrow."

His head felt very lonely without his hat as he walked home sadly to Sesame Street.

Ernie came back the next day to look for his hat. He came back the day after that, and the day after that, too. And every day Ernie looked in a different place.

He looked under park benches and picnic tables and trash cans. He looked over fences and hedges and gates. Ernie looked around and through and in everything he could think of, but he did not find his hat.

"I give up," Ernie said, sighing, and he sat down under a large oak tree. Just then a robin began to sing. Ernie looked up and saw the robin in the tree. He also saw...his hat!

"I'm coming to save you," Ernie called to his hat, and he climbed up the tree as quickly as he could. But when he reached the limb, there was something in Ernie's hat, and it was not a head. "Bert will never believe this!" said Ernie. The robin had built a nest in Ernie's hat, and in the nest were three beautiful blue eggs.

"What a silly nest!" said Ernie. "I can't take my hat back until the mother robin's eggs are hatched."

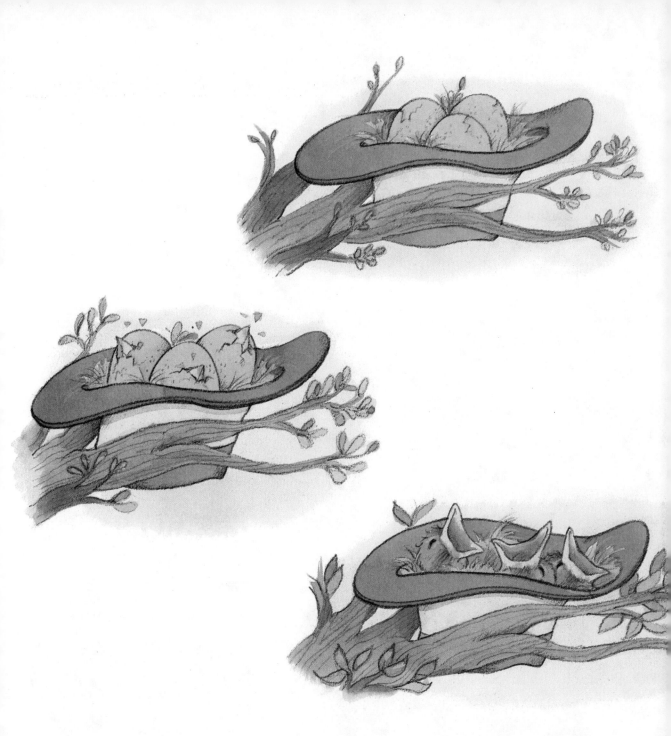

So every day Ernie went to the park to visit his hat. Soon he saw cracks in the eggshells. Then he saw beaks breaking through the cracks. Finally the baby robins came out of the shells.

"Wow!" said Ernie. "I can't take my hat back until the baby birds are bigger."

So Ernie sat in the tree and watched as the mother bird brought her babies wiggly worms to eat. *Cheep, cheep,* the baby birds sang.

All summer Ernie waited and Ernie watched. The baby birds grew bigger and stronger.

"I can't take my hat back until the babies are big enough and strong enough to fly away," he said.

Summer was almost over, and the days were growing shorter. The leaves began to turn red and orange and yellow.

Then one day when Ernie went to visit his hat, the oak tree was quiet. The nest was empty.

Ernie sat in the tree and waited, but the birds did not come.

"The bird family must have gone to a warm place for the winter," said Ernie sadly.

"Well, at least I can have my hat back now!" he said.

Ernie carried the hat down from the tree. He shook out all the twigs. And out fell a long, beautiful feather.

"Bert will never believe this!" said Ernie. "The birds left a present for me." And he put the feather in the band of his hat.

The wind was blowing as Ernie walked home to Sesame Street, and this time he held on to his hat.

A Short Story
by *Little Bird*

If you are little,
If you are small,
If you're not big,
And not very tall,

You can fit into
Very small places,
Out-of-the-way,
Snuggly spaces.

If you are small,
It is easy to send
Your little self to
Your very best friend.

If you are little,
You can sleep anywhere—
A drawer or a slipper,
Or under a chair.

When you are little,
Traveling's easy to do.
In a pocket or backpack
You have a great view.

When you are little,
Small foods are the best—
Serve raisins and peas
To your little guest.